DISCARD

JUN - - 2009

ORLAND PARK PUBLIC LIBRARY
14921 RAVINIA AVENUE
ORLAND PARK, ILLINOIS 60462
708-428-5100

Big Cat Pepper

Elizabeth Partridge
illustrated by Lauren Castillo

BLOOMSBURY
NEW YORK BERLIN LONDON

ORLAND PARK PUBLIC LIBRARY

E
PAR

Text copyright © 2009 by Elizabeth Partridge
Illustrations copyright © 2009 by Lauren Castillo
All rights reserved. No part of this book may be used or reproduced
in any manner whatsoever without written permission from the publisher,
except in the case of brief quotations embodied in critical articles or reviews.

Published by Bloomsbury U.S.A. Children's Books
175 Fifth Avenue, New York, New York 10010

Library of Congress Cataloging-in-Publication Data
Partridge, Elizabeth.
Big Cat Pepper / by Elizabeth Partridge ; illustrated by Lauren Castillo. — 1st U.S. ed.
p. cm.
Summary: Big Cat Pepper has always been part of the family,
but after he grows very old and dies, the boy who loves him comes to understand
his mother's reassurance that "his spirit is forever and can fly, fly, fly."
ISBN-13: 978-1-59990-024-7 • ISBN-10: 1-59990-024-6 (hardcover)
ISBN-13: 978-1-59990-374-3 • ISBN-10: 1-59990-374-1 (reinforced)
[1. Stories in rhyme. 2. Cats—Fiction. 3. Death—Fiction.] I. Castillo, Lauren, ill. II. Title.
PZ8.3.P27145Big 2009 [E]—dc22 2008039894

Art created with mixed media
Typeset in Horley Old Style
Book design by Nicole Gastonguay

First U.S. Edition 2009
Printed in China
2 4 6 8 10 9 7 5 3 1 (hardcover)
2 4 6 8 10 9 7 5 3 1 (reinforced)

All papers used by Bloomsbury U.S.A. are natural, recyclable products
made from wood grown in well-managed forests. The manufacturing processes
conform to the environmental regulations of the country of origin.

To my sisters and brothers,
Joan, Josh, Meg, and Aaron —E. P.

For my family, in memory of our Chauncy —L. C.

Mama, me, and Pepper,
always been this way.
Never been without him,
even for a day.

After school I look for him
where he likes to rest,
underneath our apple tree
in his grassy nest.

Sometimes I don't find him,
but I've got a secret trick.

I just shake his kibble bag,
and he comes running quick.

One day he didn't follow me
when I tried to play.
He didn't want much dinner,
just hid himself away.

I made a little soft place
and snuggled Pepper in.
I wrapped my arms around him
and stroked his furry chin.

5067835
ORLAND PARK PUBLIC LIBRARY

After school the next week,
he quit his rumbly purr.
Wouldn't drink his water
or lick his stripy fur.

Please purr, Pepper.
Please purr, purr.

But Big Cat Pepper is way too old.

Is he gonna die, Mama,
is he gonna die?
Mama said she thought so,
cry, oh cry.

I check him in the morning,
Mama was right.
Mama lets me stay home,
heart shut tight.

We put him in the flower bed,
way down deep.

We cover him with blossoms,
just like sleep.

Will he be afraid, Mama,
way down deep?

No, sugar, no,
I'll tell you why.
His spirit is forever—
it can fly, fly, fly.

Evenings are so lonely,
bedtime is the worst.

So full-up with sadness,
I think I'm gonna burst.

I think about Pepper
every single day.
The aching in my chest
never goes away.

One summer morning
near Pepper's favorite tree,
I puzzle out what Mama means
by spirit flying free.

If I stand real quiet,
will I see his spirit fly?
Big Cat Pepper,
I'm gonna try.

Grass tickling on my legs
feels like Pepper's fur.
In the wind that whispers,
I can hear him purr.

Breeze plays around me,
clouds roll by.
My heart flies open,
can't say why.

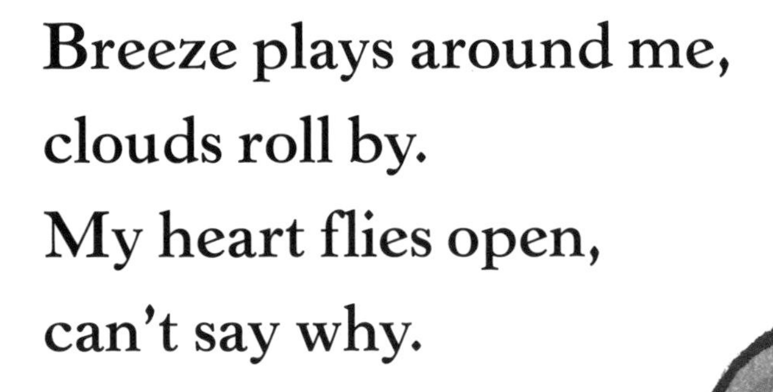

"Pepper," I whisper, "you're always in my heart."

Now I know for sure we'll never be apart.

ORLAND PARK PUBLIC LIBRARY